Sabrina Sue
Loves the Mountains

written and illustrated by
Priscilla Burris

Ready-to-Read

Simon Spotlight

New York   London   Toronto   Sydney   New Delhi

For Debbie & Phil Beck,
Kathy & Bob Alexander, and Jennifer Henn

SIMON SPOTLIGHT
An imprint of Simon & Schuster Children's Publishing Division
1230 Avenue of the Americas, New York, New York 10020
This Simon Spotlight edition December 2024
Copyright © 2024 by Priscilla Burris
All rights reserved, including the right of reproduction in whole
or in part in any form.
SIMON SPOTLIGHT, READY-TO-READ, and colophon are registered
trademarks of Simon & Schuster, LLC.
Simon & Schuster: Celebrating 100 Years of Publishing in 2024
For information about special discounts for bulk purchases, please contact
Simon & Schuster Special Sales at 1-866-506-1949
or business@simonandschuster.com.
The Simon & Schuster Speakers Bureau can bring authors to your live event. For more
information or to book an event contact the Simon & Schuster Speakers Bureau
at 1-866-248-3049 or visit our website at www.simonspeakers.com.
Manufactured in the United States of America 1124 LAK
2 4 6 8 10 9 7 5 3 1
CIP data for this book is available from the Library of Congress.
ISBN 978-1-6659-4788-6 (hc)
ISBN 978-1-6659-4787-9 (pbk)
ISBN 978-1-6659-4789-3 (ebook)

Sabrina Sue lived on a farm.
She liked to walk through
the fields.
One morning in the distance
she saw—
a big, tall mountain!

Sabrina Sue daydreamed.

I want to go to that mountain!

I want to climb to the top, she thought.

She told her farm friends her idea.

Sabrina Sue thought and thought.

Should I not go? Is it too high?

I really want to climb that mountain.

I do not mind if it is scary.

I am brave.

I will be a mountain climber!

She practiced climbing.
Soon she was ready to go.

She got up onto Farmer Martha's truck.

She plopped into a cozy corner.

The truck went up and down and around and around.

Sabrina Sue slid to the ground.

It was a dusty walk to the mountain.

Sabrina Sue climbed up with a rope.

Hiking is fun!

Sabrina Sue was happy to be back on the farm.
But one day she would visit the mountain again!